© 1992 by the Estate of Dayal Kaur Khalsa

All rights reserved. No part of this work may be reproduced or transmitted in any form or by any means, electronic or mechanical, including photocopying and recording, or by any information storage and retrieval system, without permission in writing from the publisher.

Published in Canada by Tundra Books, Montreal, Quebec H3Z 2N2

Published in the United States by Clarkson Potter Publishers, New York, 10022

Canadian Cataloging in Publication Data:

Khalsa, Dayal Kaur, (1943 — 1989)
    The Snow Cat

ISBN 0-88776-293-X

    I. Title.

PS8571.H36S6   1992   jC813'.54   C92-090241-3
PZ7.K48Sn   1992

Summary: Elsie, who lives alone in a snow-covered house on the edge of the woods, makes a friend when a huge cat of snow comes to play with her.

Design by Howard Klein

Printed in Hong Kong by South China Printing Co. Ltd.

First Canadian Edition

THE SNOW CAT

DAYAL   KAUR   KHALSA

Tundra Books

Have you ever lived alone at the edge of the woods in the middle of winter? When the snow is piled so high the eaves of the roof are a handspan away and you can break off icicles like crystal carrots? When endless, creamy fields of snow pour over the countryside, dolloping the horizon with little hills, already blurry again with new snow falling?

And the only sounds you hear are the howling wind at night and the whisper of fresh snow slithering against the windowpanes? Or, in the glistening day, you listen to the fairy tinkle of your snowshoes as you make long loops through the fields following rabbit tracks?

And the only face you ever see is your own, when, at the turn of the stairs each night you hold the candle aloft and catch a glimpse of yourself in the sleek black window, wavering like the moon fallen into a well?

If you have ever lived this way, then you know what a very lonely life it can be. And you can sympathize with Elsie, who lived alone in a little house at the edge of the woods—and you can understand how one night she knelt down before the blazing wood stove and prayed, with all her might, to God to give her a cat to keep her company: "Dear God, oh, how I would love a nice big cat to share my little house. I haven't even a morsel to give it to eat, but how I'd love a nice big cat to warm my feet at night. Perhaps you could send me an unhungry cat."

It happened that it was a particularly good night for praying. The cold night sky swirled overhead with millions of star-holes twinkling from the brilliant light of heaven beyond. As you know, on such clear wintery nights in the country, prayers, like the tall gray feathers of wood smoke sticking up out of farmhouse chimneys, rise especially straight up to God.

God heard Elsie's prayer and immediately set to work making her a nice big cat out of snow.

He used icicles for the teeth and bones, and hailstones for the eyes. He rounded it out with fresh, fluffy snow. When the Snow Cat was just the shape he wanted, God blew gently on the Snow Cat's belly until it began to rise and fall in rhythm with His own breath—and the Snow Cat slowly came alive.

He sent it down to earth in a snowstorm.

Elsie lay in bed listening to the storm. The shutters clattered, the windows rattled, and the wind dove down the chimney so sharply that the ashes heaped at the bottom of the big wood stove chased each other around in little gray circles of confusion.

The Snow Cat had landed.

It was almost as big as a cow.

"My, what a terrible storm this is," said Elsie, yawning. "I think I'll just go back to sleep and worry about it in the morning."

The Snow Cat was also yawning. He was tired from his long journey. He curled into a big ball of snow and fell asleep, purring like an avalanche.

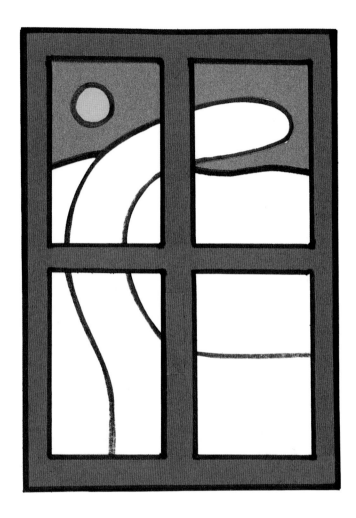

In the morning when Elsie went down to light the stove, she saw what looked like a whole hill of snow piled against the window. She thought she had been snowed in. But a few minutes later the window was clear.

"Strange," she thought. And when she looked again, there was just a tall thin pillar of snow wagging against the sky. "This is very curious," said Elsie.

She stepped outside to see what was happening.

There stood an enormous cat made out of snow.

"Meow," he said and stepped cautiously toward her. He gave her a good sniff. Then he rubbed against her shoulder. "Meow."

Elsie could hardly believe her eyes. Her prayers had been answered. And in such a big way! She reached out hesitantly and patted the Snow Cat's head.

"Meow," he said again. She scratched behind his huge ear. The Snow Cat started to purr gently. Elsie threw her arms around the Snow Cat's neck. She was so happy!

Then the Snow Cat began to meow very, very loudly. He arched his neck and his brow furrowed.

"Meow, meow, meow!" said the Snow Cat. "*Meow!*"

"Oh no!" said Elsie. "He's hungry. What am I to do? I don't even have food for a little cat, and look at the size of this one!"

Nevertheless, she went into the house and brought out what little food she had. She put a bowl of soup before him. The Snow Cat sniffed it and turned away. She held out a shiny apple. The Snow Cat put his nose in the air. She offered him a crust of bread. He let it fall to the snow and scowled. "Meow, meow, meow, meow, meow!" howled the Snow Cat.

"Oh dear me," wailed Elsie. "The poor thing is starving. What shall I do?"

A light snow began to fall. God's voice called down, "Try snow."

"Snow?"

"Snow!" shouted God, and then all was quiet.

Elsie was perplexed. "What is He talking about?"

"Think!" said the huge voice.

Elsie thought. And soon enough she had it. "Of course," she said. "Snow cats eat snow food!"

She got her shovel and began sculpting delicious food out of snow: big wedges of cream cheese, bottles of milk and bowls of sour cream, fish sticks, plump little white mice—everything a snow cat would love.

The Snow Cat gobbled it all up.

There are certain days that are the very best days—days that are even better than birthdays. These are the days on which you make a new friend—and discover the world together.

Elsie took the Snow Cat to all her favorite places and showed him everything she loved: the white flowing fields, the magic evergreen woods, and the crooked fence about the top of the hill.

They rolled down the slopes and climbed the copper-colored apple trees. They marveled at the delicate gray-green lichen that grew on the pink boulders in the valley. Elsie laughed and the Snow Cat purred and they played all day long.

Then suddenly evening came like an uninvited guest, draping its purple cloak too soon on the bare black trees rimming the hill, whispering coldly, *Night again.* Elsie said to the Snow Cat, "We'd better hurry home before it gets too dark."

They were just about to enter the snug little house when a terrible whirlwind of snow blew up. The sky turned white and God's voice roared, "Stop! Elsie—listen carefully: I have given you the Snow Cat to keep you company through the long winter. But you must never take the Snow Cat into your warm little house. Do you understand?"

"Y-y-yes, sir."

"And do you promise to do as I say?"

"Yes, sir. B-b-but what about the long lonely evenings all alone by the fire?"

God roared louder than ever, "Never take the Snow Cat into your house!"

Then the whirlwind died down and the snowflakes fell to the ground, sparkling like diamonds. Elsie patted the Snow Cat's head and hugged him tight.

"You'll have to stay out here tonight," she said, and, making him a few last sardines, she bid him good night.

As Elsie sat alone by the blazing wood stove, it seemed to her that she felt even lonelier than before. She looked wistfully out the window at the Snow Cat sitting up on the hill. He was looking down at the house. She wished so much he could be at her side.

The Snow Cat was lonely too. Sadly he walked down the hill to the little house. He sniffed at the door and rubbed against the corners. He pressed his big nose against the window and meowed. Elsie and the Snow Cat looked at each other longingly.

"Perhaps if you just came in for a very little while," said Elsie, "and then went right back outside again, it would be all right."

The Snow Cat nodded his head in happy agreement.

Elsie threw open the door and the Snow Cat pranced inside.

How happy they were! Elsie settled down in her big soft chair by the fire, sipping a cup of creamy cocoa. The Snow Cat curled up at her feet, purring contentedly. It was so calm and cozy in the little house, and they felt so happy and peaceful together that before they knew it, both Elsie and the Snow Cat fell fast asleep.

Outside the cold wind whistled. A sliver of moon rode the dark clouds like a little canoe lost on a vast black lake.

At dawn the sky was streaked with red. Elsie woke with a start. Something was not right! Her feet were freezing cold—and wet!

She jumped up, terrified. The floor was covered with water!

Filled with dread, she followed that stream of water as it poured out her door and rushed down the hill. Her heart felt like stone. She followed the icy water all the way down. At the bottom, in the little valley, was a newly formed pond, already frozen over. It was exactly the shape of the Snow Cat.

Elsie had never felt so miserable in all her life. She fell to her knees at the edge of the pond and cried her heart out.

A gentle breeze blew up and dried the tears upon her cheeks. God's voice said, "Elsie, do not be sad. The Snow Cat can still be your friend. But in a different way. You can still have fun with him. Go get your ice skates." "Yes sir," said Elsie bravely.

There was no joy in her heart as she laced up her skates. Skating wasn't any fun. But she kept on and as the day passed, little by little, Elsie began to feel better. Until at last she was actually enjoying doing her figure eights and pirouettes. Every day that winter Elsie went to the pond and skated with her friend, the Snow Cat.

When spring came the ice melted and from the pond came a symphony of
sounds: fish splashing, the humming of blue darning needles' wings, the croaking
of frogs. She brought her canoe to the pond and paddled around. In the evenings
she sat beside the Snow Cat pond and listened to the music of the new season.

When summer came she put on her bathing suit and swam in the Snow Cat pond.
She *was* still having fun with her friend.

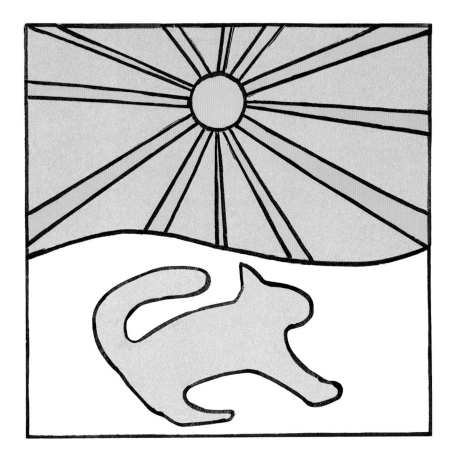

As for the Snow Cat, he actually thrived living out in the fresh country air. Every spring there were more and more frogs and fishes splashing about him. And every summer the wild-flowers and berry bushes crowned his banks like a garland. In the autumn, geese stopped and rested on their way down south. And in the long winter evenings the sound of the wind wrapped itself around the warm little house like a giant happy cat purring contentedly.

And do you know, even to this very day, if you go to the edge of the woods and find that little house, and follow the path from its door to the little valley, you will still find the Snow Cat—sparkling like a diamond in the sun.

ABOUT THE AUTHOR

The enormously gifted author and illustrator Dayal Kaur Khalsa died in 1989 at the age of forty-six. In some way, she must have known that her time was short, for her output in the last years of her life was astonishing. Seven books were written and illustrated in just six years: *Tales of a Gambling Grandma, I Want a Dog, Sleepers, My Family Vacation, How Pizza Came to Our Town, Julian,* and *Cowboy Dreams*.

One of Dayal Kaur's favorite works, *The Snow Cat*, remained unpublished at the time of her death. In 1991, her longtime friend, artist Brian Grison, rediscovered the original paintings done for *The Snow Cat* many years ago and brought them from Toronto to New York—much to the delight of her agent and publisher. Friends, fans, and new readers will find this story one of Dayal Kaur Khalsa's most memorable.

She also left a beautiful series of cowboy paintings; the poet Mark Strand is writing a story to go with them.